Angelina, Prima Ballerina

Visit our website at:
www.autumnchildrensbooks.co.uk

Angelina Ballerina was a star at her school, Camembert Academy, but she wanted to shine even brighter!

"I wish I could dance like I was floating on air!"
Angelina declared during practice. She raised
her arms over her head and pirouetted through
Ms. Mimi's classroom.

Angelina stopped and stared at her favourite
photograph in the classroom. It was of the older
students dancing in a ballet recital.

"I wish I could dance like the older ballerinas,"
Angelina told her friend, Alice. She began to twirl.
"One *chaîné!* Two *chaînés!* Three..."

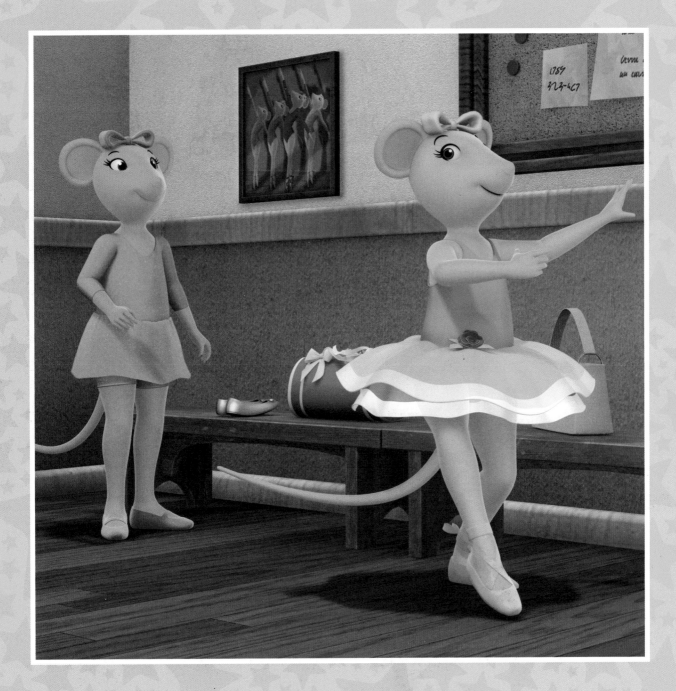

Oops! Angelina twirled straight into Alice and they both fell to the floor!

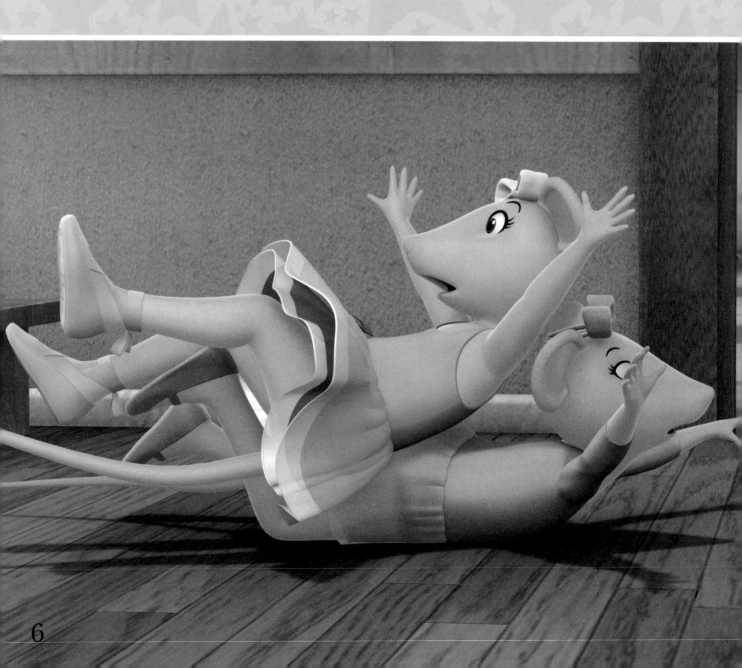

Angelina looked up and saw her friend Marco standing in the doorway.

"I picked out a new instrument to play and it's just arrived," he told his friends. "It has strings like a violin but it's much bigger!" Angelina and Alice couldn't wait to see it!

Angelina twirled down the hall and bumped into her teacher, Ms. Mimi, who was hanging up a poster. Angelina looked closer and saw that it was a notice for auditions for the Mousnikov Ballet.

Angelina's heart pirouetted. Dancing with the Mousnikov Ballet would be a dream come true!

But the dancers in the Mousnikov Ballet wore pointe shoes, and Ms. Mimi didn't think Angelina was ready for those. The auditions were for the older students.

Angelina said goodbye to Ms. Mimi and hurried away to see Marco and his new instrument.

The instrument was a huge string bass. It was so big that Marco had to stand on a chair to play it.

"I guess it will take practice," Marco decided, as he tried to play the huge bass.

"Practice!" Angelina gasped. Marco had given her an idea.

Angelina went to the lost and found box. *Voilà!* She pulled out a pair of satin shoes with a hard, flat toe, just like the older dancers wore.

After school, Alice went to Angelina's house. Angelina showed Alice her new shoes. With her friend's help, Angelina performed an arabesque!

"Maybe I can try out for the ballet after all!" cried Angelina.

Angelina brought her shoes to school the next
day, but every time she let go of the barre,
she fell down.

Angelina's legs and feet were sore from falling
down so often.

Mrs. Mouseling thought Angelina should stay at home to rest, but Angelina didn't want to miss the audition.

The next day, Angelina's legs felt strong enough to dance. She was still very nervous, though!

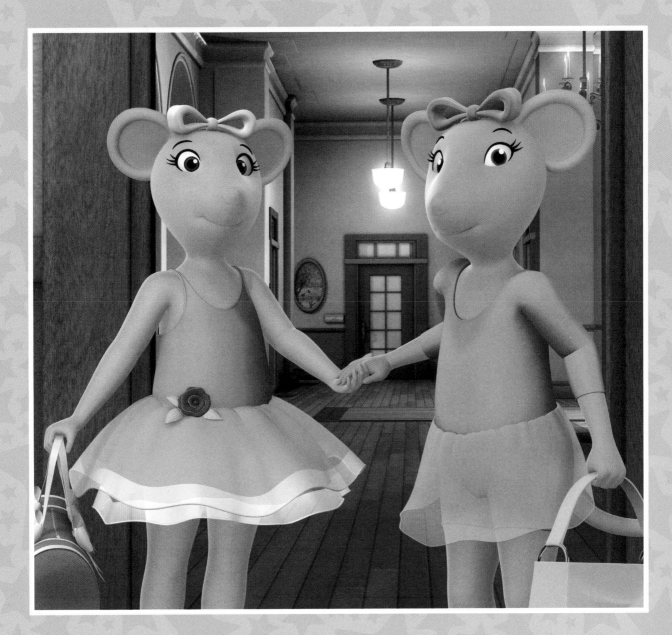

Before the auditions were due to start, Angelina and Alice went to the music room to find Marco with his huge string bass.

"I can't play this instrument," Marco said with a sigh, "It's just too big."

As they were standing there, Ms. Mimi came into the room with a much smaller instrument. There had been a mistake; this was Marco's instrument. It was the perfect size for him!

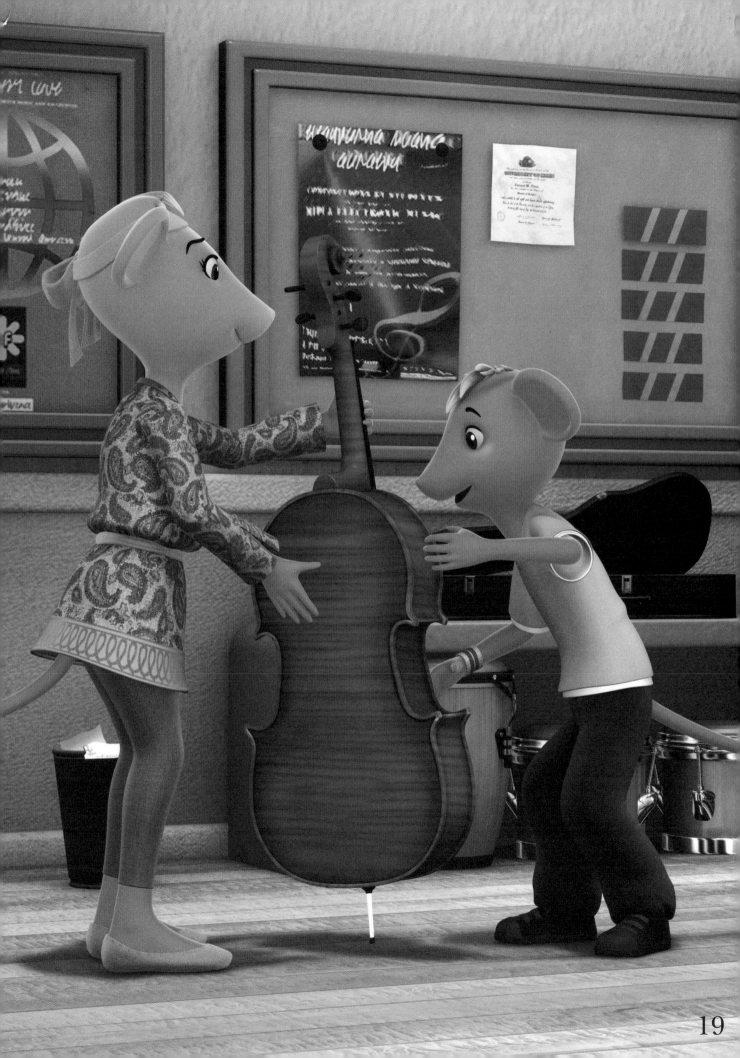

Soon it was time for the Mousnikov Ballet audition!

Angelina raced to the dance studio and put on her special shoes.

Angelina's legs wobbled as she tried to walk.
She fell straight into Ms. Mimi's classroom!
Ms. Mimi came over to see if she was okay.
    "I really want to be a prima ballerina,"
Angelina told her teacher. "But I don't think I can."

"Yes, you can," Ms. Mimi told Angelina. "You just need a few more years of practice."

Angelina knew that Ms. Mimi was right. Just like Marco and his instrument, dancers had to be the right size, too! Until then, Angelina would just keep dreaming her big dreams.